THE SPECIAL GUEST

A CHRISTMAS STORY

THE SPECIAL GUEST

A CHRISTMAS STORY

Written by:

LEE ALLEN

Illustrated by:

DONNA ALLEN

SCHOLASTIC INC.

New York Toronto London Auckland Sydney

ISBN 0-590-99525-1

12 11 10 9 8 7 6 5 4 3   7 8 9/9 0 1/0

Printed in the U.S.A.   40
First Scholastic printing, December 1996

A special thanks to Tom Wright with editing assistance that went beyond what one could ask of a friend.

This story was originally written as
a Christmas gift to my beautiful children,
Justin and Ellie, the delight of my heart.

—*Their father*

To err is human, to forgive divine.

—Alexander Pope

Prologue

The holiday scene in Richmond, Virginia, was hectic that last shopping day before Christmas. Bumper to bumper traffic stringed the lengths of streets like toy cars on Santa's assembly line, while sidewalks overflowed with shoppers dressed as colorfully as sprinkles on Christmas cookies. People passed one another with friendly but harried expressions as they darted in and out of stores, some with children in tow, while others had stolen away alone to buy that special someone a gift. Meanwhile all of Richmond was in a hurry-scurry to finish their Christmas lists before closing time.

Throughout the day, as the temperature had dropped and the clouds had turned a chalky gray, the City had huddled together to speculate about a white Christmas. The change in weather had brought a change of mood in Richmonders. It was as if the North wind now blowing through the streets had blown in a spirit of good cheer. There was an excitement of that peculiar kind found only in the South, when snow is in the air, and adults are transformed into children as they shut down their normal routines to go traipsing through the snow or retreat to a crackling fire with a mug of hot cinnamon cider.

That it was Christmas weekend made the prospects for snow all the more special. A charm had settled over the city, where the everyday Scrooges were now nicer and the usual cacophony of city noises more harmonious, as if a symphony were playing. Even the honking horn of an impatient driver no longer irritated so much as added a metaphor, like a well-timed, clashing cymbal, to the Christmas music pealing from shops and shoppers' hearts. And so, though the day was as hectic as a houseful of grandchildren on Christmas morning, it was a day heartily embraced by everyone.

Meanwhile, in the midst of all the bustle, one lone figure moved along patiently, oblivious to the crowd. Stopping, he pulled out his pocket watch then, with a nod, clasped the watch shut and settled into a nearby seat; it was almost time. He had travelled a great distance to come to Richmond and, now, his mission for this Christmas was about to begin.

I

Scott Reid observed the crowded parking lot with a growing annoyance. From his vantage, it seemed the whole city was out shopping for food this Saturday. He knew that was because there were only a few hours remaining to stock up for Christmas—at least for Food-Krop's customers. To-morrow was Christmas Eve, and Food-Krop's Super Markets would be closed, as they always were on Sunday.

He frowned as he weaved his grocery cart through a row of cars. Thinking about the holidays had only made him more depressed today. Not because it was one of the busiest times of the year at his job either. No, he grimaced, it was because today marked the anniversary and, all day long, fresh memories of the accident had flashed through his mind.

At the moment he was busy working his job as a courtesy clerk, which was just a modern title for an old-fashioned bag boy. Scott worked at the Food-Krop's market in Carytown. A popular shopping district in Richmond, Carytown nestled inside a half dozen city blocks like an old village. The vin-tage shops were reminiscent of an era predating malls and superstores and famous locally for offering a variety of wares that could rival a giant bazaar.

His thoughts drifted back to the present. Right now he was making, by his estimation, his *one thousandth* trip to a customer's car. Not just any customer, he reminded himself. It was Mrs. Brigglesworth, one of the bigwigs in the local garden club and his Sunday school teacher from grade school years.

At the moment Mrs. B., as she was known to everyone, was chattering like a magpie about something or other. Back in Sunday school, Scott had learned how to tune Mrs. B. out while not missing anything she said that was too important. Right now he was practicing his old talent, finding her blue tinted hair far more interesting than the conversation.

As a youngster, he had wondered why Mrs. B.'s hair was blue. One day his mother had explained that Mrs. B. dyed it. Scott shook his head with a smile. To this day, her choice of colors remained a mystery. Now as he followed behind, groceries in tow, he watched her hair sparkle and tried to think what it reminded him of. Blue cotton candy perhaps?

There was a lull. She had asked him a question. "Ma'am?" he asked.

Mrs. B. slowed down so he could catch up. "You're not a daydreamer still, are you Scott?" She was teasing him.

"Sorry, Mrs. B, I didn't hear you."

"I said, 'Will you be attending the live nativity at church tomorrow night?' "

"I'm in the play."

"Are you now?" She looked pleased. "What part?"

"I'm one of the wise men. Actually, I'll be riding the camel this year," he added proudly.

"How'd you manage that?"

"We drew straws, and I was the lucky one."

Scott's church had used the camel Penelope in their play for years. He was sure the exotic animal was one reason the play was such a popular attraction in Richmond. Each year only one wise man was selected to ride Penelope, and this year it had been him. Scott smiled to himself. He was glad that his parents had insisted he try out for the part, because riding Penelope was like being a celebrity.

"It couldn't have happened to a nicer person!" she patted him. "Did you know I was in our church's first live nativity?"

He shook his head.

"I was. I played Mother Mary and my husband, Fred, played Joseph. That was Christmas 1945, the year World War II ended. I remember because Fred and the other boys in his unit had just returned from Europe. He served in Virginia's 'Blue Ridge Division,' you know. Saw action in the Battle of the Bulge too," she added proudly.

Mrs. B. stopped talking long enough to pop the trunk of her car. "While you're loading the groceries, I'll tell you a funny story about that first play."

As he started filling the trunk with grocery bags, Scott glanced at Mrs. B. Her eyes had a faraway look, as she hugged her purse close.

"That was the first year we started using real animals," she began. "Someone got the idea the Christmas story would be more memorable for the children that way, which it was. We got permission from the preacher, then made arrangements to borrow some barnyard animals from Jack Snead, a farmer in the church. One of the animals was a cow.

"Well, everything was going fine the night of the performance until that cow decided to walk the aisles. Somehow she found Jack Snead seated in the congregation and started nudging him with her nose and mooing and carrying on to beat the band." Mrs. B. started to chuckle. "Probably she was saying she wanted to go home!

"Anyway, at first everyone tried to keep a straight face as Reverend Stodges read from the Bible. Jack, meanwhile, tried to discreetly lead his cow back to the manger scene. Yet no sooner did he get her situated and start walking back to his seat than she trotted after him." Mrs. B.'s eyes danced with merriment. "There I was rocking Baby Jesus and trying not to laugh while Jack tugged on his cow, her neck stretching like a rubber band while her feet refused to budge an inch. It was a hoot!

"As you can imagine, the audience couldn't restrain themselves. The whole church broke into laughter right in the middle of the play. Even Reverend Stodges, who was always the formal sort, joined in the fun. I don't think I ever laughed so hard as that night!"

"What happened to the cow, Mrs. B.?"

"Jack finally got her outside. But by then she had stolen the show! Somehow we still managed to talk the preacher into using animals the next year. After that, it was a tradition. And now," she nudged him, "we even use a camel."

"Yep," Scott grinned. He had finished loading the groceries and was leaning on his cart enjoying Mrs. B.'s story.

"By the way," her tone became serious, "how's your sister doing?"

Feeling his stomach tighten at the question, he straightened up. "She's still the same."

"You know, I had a dream the other night that Jenny recovered. It was a strange dream, though now I can barely remember the details." Mrs. B.'s voice lowered. "When I woke up, I just knew it meant something." She studied him. "You believe your sister is going to recover, don't you Scott?"

Lots of people with good intentions had tried to be encouraging during the past year, like Mrs. B. was doing now, but he was beginning to have his doubts. "I guess," he answered, looking down to hide the hurt he felt.

Mrs. B. tried to look him in the eye. "You don't sound too convinced."

Scott shrugged as he stared at the pavement.

"Don't you worry," she patted his arm, "your sister's going to be fine. Just you watch!"

A gust of wind suddenly whipped across the parking lot, throwing them both off balance. "Brrrr," Mrs. B. shivered and pulled her overcoat tight at the neck. "Think the weatherman is right about a white Christmas?"

Scott looked up at the sky. All afternoon he had watched the clouds turning grayer. Thinking of snow now brightened his mood. "I sure hope so!"

"Me too," she winked, sliding behind the wheel of her car. "A white Christmas is magical."

Pushing his cart back to the store, Scott noticed a shiny, old car which was double parked. He pushed alongside and peered into the driver's window. The interior was in perfect condition.

He found the name Packard in chrome letters on the back trunk. Well, he had never heard of that make. Lingering for a minute, he walked around the car and admired the sleek aerodynamics, the oversized wheel wells, and all the shiny chrome. "Boy, to have a car like this!" he whistled. "What would the guys at school say?" Scott already knew he wanted a classic for his first car, instead of one of those newer models.

A horn suddenly jolted him back to the present. Remembering that his fellow courtesy clerks would be looking for him, he gave the car a last admiring glance, then hustled toward the store. Today wasn't a day to dawdle.

He was about to pass through the store's sliding doors when, out of the corner of his eye, something caught his attention. There was someone sitting at the outdoor cafe. It was a man reading a book.

Outside in this weather? He must be crazy, Scott thought to himself, shaking his head.

The weather had turned so cold that, by now, Scott was wearing several layers of clothing underneath his Food-

Krop's apron. At least the man was wearing an overcoat and hat. It was one of those old-fashioned kinds of hats, a Homburg, he had heard it called, like his great-grandfather wore in photographs at home. In fact, this man looked like he could be from his great-grandfather's era.

The stranger must have sensed Scott staring because he suddenly raised his head and gave Scott a quizzical look. Embarrassed to be caught staring, Scott nodded to the man and quickly pushed his cart inside the store.

The brief encounter with the stranger gave Scott a strange feeling that tugged at him throughout the afternoon. As he carted groceries out to customers' cars, Scott found himself glancing over at the cafe tables to see if the man was still there. Strangely enough, he would be sitting there one time, then gone the next. The scenario repeated itself throughout the afternoon.

Finally it was nearly ten o'clock, and the store was about to close. Once again, the man had returned. Scott's curiosity was getting the best of him, because something didn't make sense. What was the man doing outside? He didn't look homeless. Yet, who in his right mind would stay outside in this cold? *Maybe he has Alzheimer's!* Scott suddenly realized. He had heard stories of old people with the disease getting lost and wandering around the neighborhood.

He decided he had better check on the man before the store closed. The man could freeze to death if he stayed outside overnight. Besides, Scott knew he wouldn't shake the strange feeling he had until he got an answer.

Mustering up his confidence Scott walked over and stood in front of the man. When the man didn't look up, Scott awkwardly cleared his throat and said, "Excuse me, Sir."

This time Scott felt alert eyes studying him from beneath a set of bushy, snow white eyebrows.

"I was by here earlier," Scott explained hesitantly.

"Yes, I remember," the man replied pleasantly.

Well, he seems friendly enough, Scott thought with relief. "I was wondering if you needed any help?"

"That depends." The stranger seemed to give Scott another appraising look as he added, "Can you fix a car?"

For years Scott had helped his father work on the family vehicles in their garage, which they had converted into a mechanic's shop. "Maybe," he shrugged back. "Where are you parked?"

"Over there." The man stood and pointed to the Packard Scott had admired earlier. It now gleamed under the bright lights in the parking lot.

"That's your car?" Scott asked excitedly.

The man nodded.

"It's a beaut! I was noticing it earlier this afternoon. How old is it?"

"She's a 1949. Runs like a top too . . . well, usually," the man smiled, correcting himself.

"Do you know what the problem is?"

"Afraid I don't know a thing about mechanics. Once in a while Charity—that's her name—starts to tucker out when we're on a long trip. When that happens I know it's time to pull over. This afternoon I barely got into the parking lot before she conked out on me. Haven't been able to get her going since."

Scott listened with amusement at the way the man talked about his car as if it were a person.

The stranger continued, "Usually, if I let her rest a while, she'll start right up." He shook his head. "Not today. I've been trying off and on for hours now."

That explained why the man kept disappearing from the cafe. He had been checking his car. Well, at least he wasn't crazy. Scott felt relieved about that.

Briskly rubbing his gloves together, Scott tried to think.

It was too late to call a garage. They were all closed by now. Definitely, he didn't feel comfortable checking out that antique automobile by himself. Then he remembered. "My dad is picking me up tonight. He knows lots about cars. I'll bet he can help."

The man's face lit up. "You think so?"

"Sure." Scott nodded enthusiastically.

"I would be grateful."

Scott suddenly realized he had not introduced himself. "By the way, my name is Scott Reid."

The man tipped the corner of his hat. "Pleased to meet you, Scott, mine's Zachery."

"Aren't you freezing, Mr. Zachery? You've been outside for hours."

"No *mister*, just Zachery," the man corrected with a smile, looking up at the sky, as though he was noticing the weather for the first time. "I see what you mean. Guess I wasn't paying any attention to the cold, what with reading my book." He held up a tattered, leather bound edition that looked to be a hundred years old. "Ever read any Charles Dickens?"

"We had to read *Great Expectations* in school."

"This is his Christmas story. It's called *A Christmas Carol.*"

"You mean the story about Scrooge?"

"The same. Have you read it?"

"I've seen the movie," Scott offered.

"No, no." The man shook his head. "That's not the same as reading the book. You need to read the book. It's a wonderful tale, one of my favorites. Never tire of reading it either. It keeps the true meaning of Christmas fresh."

As he spoke, the man unbuttoned his overcoat, revealing a bright red vest beneath, and slipped a gold pocket watch from a vest pocket to check the time.

"Do you have to be somewhere, Zachery?" Scott asked,

trying Zachery's name for the first time. He was used to us - ing "mister" with someone Zachery's age.

"No," Zachery said, slipping the watch back into the pocket. "It's just a habit I have. My busy schedule always keeps me checking the time."

"Well, my father should be here in just a few minutes." Scott glanced through the store windows. His coworkers were busy cleaning up and preparing to go home, as it was almost closing time. "I need to get back inside. Do you want to come in and warm up? Maybe have some coffee?"

"Thank you, no. I'll just wait here until your father ar- rives." Without another word Zachery sat down, picked up his book, and started reading as though Scott was no longer there.

"Suit yourself," Scott replied quietly with a bemused shrug.

Maybe the man is a bit odd after all, he thought, as he pushed his cart into the store. Still, there was something about Zachery he liked. He rather reminded Scott of Jimmy Stewart as the grandfather in one of those *Lassie* movies. Ex- cept for the bushy eyebrows. He finally realized who they re- minded him of—his great-grandfather.

$\mathscr{A}$ half hour later Scott saw his father pull up outside the store. He hurriedly wished his store manager a Merry Christmas, then ran out to the family van to tell his father about the stranger.

Max Reid listened patiently while his son explained Zachery's predicament, then replied, "Let's go take a look."

Parking the van, Max followed his son over to where Zachery was seated. Scott made the introductions, then watched as his father stared at the stranger for what seemed like minutes. Finally Max spoke.

"Have we met before?"

Zachery smiled. "Well, I'm not from around here, you know."

Max seemed perplexed. "It's just that you look so familiar . . . ." He scratched his head, then shrugged, "Oh, well."

"That's the car over there, Dad," Scott said, pointing.

"Hey, an old classic. What's the problem?"

As they walked over to the car, Zachery explained what

he had told Scott. Max walked around the old automobile, examining it with an appraising eye. "I haven't seen one of these in a long time." He ran his hand over the glossy finish. "What year is it?"

"She's a 1949, and her name is *Charity,* Dad," Scott answered, shooting Zachery a smile. Zachery winked back.

"Mind if I try and start it?" Max asked. Sliding behind the wheel, he made several attempts, then got out and opened the hood and with a penlight checked over the engine components. "Crank it again, Scott," he directed from under the hood.

Scott slid behind the wheel and turned the key.

"Hold the pedal down!" his father called out.

It was no good. The engine whined as long as Scott turned the key, then died. Straightening up, Max analyzed the situation. "Your battery is working. It's getting gas. And the spark plugs are getting fire." He looked at Zachery and shrugged. "Sorry, without my test equipment, I don't know what to say."

"She can be pretty temperamental," Zachery patted the fender.

Max glanced at his watch. "Problem is, everything is closed by now, and most places won't be open again until Tuesday, day after Christmas. Do you have a place to stay?"

"No," said Zachery, glancing around the parking lot uncertainly.

Scott noticed that the lot had quickly emptied. He had an idea and whispered it to his father. Max listened to his son, then nodded. "Okay. You can ask him."

Scott made the offer. "Zachery, if you need a place to stay, we have an extra room at our house."

"Oh, I couldn't impose like that. Not on Christmas weekend . . ."

"Nonsense!" Max held up his hand. "You can't stay in a hotel over Christmas. That would be downright depressing.

Besides, we have plenty of room at our house. Come enjoy Christmas weekend with the Reid family!"

Zachery studied both of them. "You're sure?"

Scott added, "My mom's a great cook."

"Hmmm, I don't get home cooking very often," Zachery mused. "Well, how can I say no to that offer?"

"Cool!" Scott beamed, glad that Zachery had accepted. "Do you have a bag, Zachery?"

"Sure do." Zachery opened the driver's door and hoisted an old leather roll bag off the back seat.

"Let me put it in the van for you," Scott offered. "Okay if I drive, Dad?"

"You bet," Max said, tossing Scott the keys.

Grateful for the opportunity to use his new driving permit, Scott selected the long route home while everyone got acquainted. Ten minutes later they pulled into the drive of a two story, white clapboard house with tall trees in the front yard. They were met by Scott's golden retriever, Beauchamps, who led them up the drive barking.

"Why don't you run and tell your mother we have company," his father suggested as they rolled to a stop.

As he dashed up the front steps, Scott called back to tell his father to make sure he introduced Zachery to Beauchamps. Inside, he found his mother in the kitchen. She was stirring dinner on the stove.

"What's all the excitement about, Scott?" she asked, turning around as he entered.

"We've got company, Mom!"

"Really? Who?"

"His name is Zachery."

His mother stared at him with a questioning look as he tried to spy over her shoulder to see what was for dinner. He was starved. "Well, where is this *Zachery?*"

"He's coming in with Dad. What's for dinner?" He lifted

the lid off the big pan and answered his own question. "Chili! All right!" Grabbing the wooden cooking spoon, Scott blew on a mouthful. Chili was one of his favorite winter meals.

The front door opened a second time. "Hullo!" Max called out.

Drying her hands on her apron, Ellen Reid followed her son to the front door. As she kissed Max hello, her eyes rested on the stranger. She had not expected someone so well dressed. Max had brought strangers home for a meal in the past, but this man did not appear to be homeless, as was usually the case.

"Scott, introduce your friend to your mother," his father prompted.

"Mom, this is Zachery."

Instead of shaking her hand, Zachery leaned over and gave her hand a kiss, like in the movies. Scott smiled as he watched his mother's reaction. Clearly, she was charmed by the stranger's gesture.

"Will you be joining us for dinner, Zachery?" she asked warmly.

"Actually, Scott and I have invited Zachery to spend the weekend with us," Max quickly explained. "He needs a place to stay."

Ellen nodded that was fine with her. The Reids had an ongoing agreement never to turn someone in need away. "You are welcome to stay with us, Zachery."

Zachery fingered his Homburg. "You're sure?"

"Of course," Ellen smiled. "Scott, will you show Zachery to the guest room upstairs? And show him the bath, so he can freshen up before dinner."

Scott grabbed Zachery's bag and bounded up the stairs in a few hops. He called to Zachery from the top landing to follow.

"Coming," Zachery called back, then turned to Max and Ellen. "You are very gracious to have me. Thank you for your hospitality." Before they could answer, he had climbed the stairs as effortlessly as Scott.

"Did you see that?" Max whistled. "He went up those steps like he was fifty years younger."

Ellen didn't seem to notice. "He's so charming," she glowed. "Where did you meet him?"

"Scott met him at Food-Krop's today."

"Why does he need a place to stay? I mean, he doesn't look homeless."

"He's not. He was travelling through Richmond when his car broke down." Max made a frown. "You know, I could swear I've seen him before."

"Really? Where?"

"That's just it, I don't know. But his face seems so familiar . . ."

"I've never had my hand kissed before," Ellen ribbed her husband playfully.

Max chuckled, "I'm glad you like him. I think Scott does too. Maybe it will help to have a guest here this weekend." His face changed to a look of concern. "How was your day?"

"Difficult," Ellen grimaced. "I relived the memories of the accident all day. How about you?"

"Yeah, the same. I can't say as that I've been looking forward to this weekend."

Ellen studied her husband's face. "Well, we can be thankful that we still have our daughter with us."

"You're right," Max nodded, his face taking on a smile as his mood changed. "Now, what can I do to help you get dinner ready?"

"Not a thing. Why don't you go say hello to Jenny while I set another place for Zachery."

III

*T*en minutes later the Reids and their guest had gathered around the dining room table. After grace, Ellen served up the chili, while Scott explained how he and Zachery had met.

"It sounds like you've had a long day," Ellen responded, giving Zachery a sympathetic look.

"I'm just grateful your son offered to help me. No one else did."

Max and Ellen shot their son proud looks, which Scott tried to shrug off, finding the attention embarrassing.

Ellen smiled at her son's modesty and continued the conversation. "What brings you here to Richmond, Zachery?"

"I was actually passing through on assignment."

"Business?"

Zachery accepted the plate of corn bread, took a piece and passed it on to Max. "You might say so. I work for a charitable organization."

"What kind of charity?" Max asked.

"My organization helps people with special needs who come to our attention."

"Like for instance?"

"Oh, it can be for any number of reasons. Most times our clients need special help with employment, a family crisis, finances . . . that sort of thing."

"You do all of that?"

Zachery nodded. "My organization provides me with all the resources I need to do my job. Actually, the fact that every case is a different challenge is what I enjoy most about my work."

"Your work sounds wonderful to me," Ellen replied.

Max agreed. "What's the name of your organization, Zachery?"

"We are funded by a private benefactor. I'm afraid he insists on anonymity."

Scott, who was wolfing down his chili, stopped eating. What Zachery was saying sounded intriguing. "So you're like a secret agent?"

Zachery chuckled. "Well, not exactly. I just try not to draw attention to myself."

Odd, Scott thought, everything about Zachery called attention to himself, whether it was his bushy eyebrows that looked like patches of cotton, or his outdated clothes—not to mention his Packard. "I couldn't help but notice you today." Scott shot Zachery a smile.

"Scott!" his mother admonished.

"Yes, you did indeed," Zachery winked. "That's okay, Ellen. I think Scott is telling me I look a bit outdated. To tell you the truth, I have trouble keeping up with all the new fads. Though you might be surprised, Scott, people are so busy these days they really don't notice me."

Max drummed his fingers on the table as he tried to think. "There was a popular show on television back in the fifties. Wasn't it called *The Millionaire,* Dear?"

"I think so. I remember I used to watch it in the after-noons with my grandmother. Why?"

"Each show, the main character—I forget his name—vis-ited someone who had been specially selected and handed them a check for *one million dollars*. The mysterious part about the show was the benefactor who stayed behind the scene, like in Zachery's organization."

"Is that what you do?" Scott asked, his eyes growing big.

"The million dollars part doesn't sound too familiar," Zachery chuckled. "I'm afraid my employer is too frugal for that." Zachery seemed amused by the conversation as he scooped up his last spoonful of chili. "This is delicious, Ellen."

"Would you care for more?"

Zachery gave an enthusiastic nod, which was quickly sec-onded by Scott and Max. While Ellen refilled their bowls, Max continued asking questions. He was intrigued about Zachery's work.

"So, I take it you travel a lot?"

"All over. I just came from Missoula."

"Missoula?" Scott frowned.

"Montana."

"You mean you drove Charity all the way out there?" Scott's eyes grew wide.

"Sure. Like I said, she's a great automobile. Just once in awhile . . ."

"Oh, Mom," Scott said, interrupting Zachery, "I forgot to tell you how old Charity is. She's a 1949 model!"

"No wonder you broke down today." Ellen's reply made the men laugh.

Turning to his father, Scott asked, "Are we going to try and work on Zachery's car tomorrow, Dad?"

"Sure. Why not."

"Wait a minute," Ellen interjected. "We have church to-morrow, remember? Then, Scott, you have dress rehearsal tomorrow afternoon for the play tomorrow night." She gave them a reproving look. "And besides, you know I don't approve of that sort of thing on Sunday."

"But Zachery needs his car," Scott protested. He didn't want to say it, but he was anxious to take a ride in the Packard. He had already thought it through. First, he was going to ask Zachery if they could take the car for a drive. Then he would see if he could find some of his friends to show it off to. Heck, none of them had ever driven a Packard—probably never even seen one. Scott smiled to himself, *Boy, will the guys be envious!*

Scott's father interrupted his thoughts. "Your mother is right, Scott." Max turned to Zachery. "That is, unless you feel pressured to leave, Zachery."

Zachery shook his head diplomatically, "It can wait."

Scott shrugged. Actually, he wasn't so sure he wanted Zachery leaving so soon anyway. He was enjoying their guest. A ride in the Packard could wait a day or so. Changing the subject, he asked, "Guess what kind of car I want, Zachery?"

"I'm afraid I don't know too much about modern cars, Scott."

"It's not a modern one. I'm talking about a classic. Like yours. Ever hear of a Bug?"

Zachery frowned. "A what?"

Scott laughed. "The little round car with the bug eyes. It's called a Volkswagen Bug. They don't make them anymore."

"No, don't think I have."

"They're really cool looking!"

Max interrupted, "Son, I've told you a car is a lot of upkeep. That's why I don't want you to even think about buying an automobile right now."

"Max, he's just being a normal sixteen-year-old," Ellen coaxed her husband with a smile. She leaned toward their guest and explained, "Scott has just acquired his driving permit." Then in a low voice, "As you can see, there's a battle of the wills going on over this car thing."

Scott made a scowl. "I shouldn't have brought it up."

Zachery cleared his throat and tactfully changed the subject. "Did I hear something about a play tomorrow night?"

Ellen explained about the church play and Scott's special part.

"How did you learn to ride a camel, Scott?" Zachery asked, obviously impressed.

"Penelope's not hard to ride. Her trainer taught me how. You just have to pretend you're riding a rocking chair."

That seemed to tickle Zachery. "You know, Scott, you and I really haven't had a chance to get acquainted, yet. I don't even know what grade you're in."

"I'm a junior."

"Tell Zachery about the writing contest you recently placed second in, Scott," his mother prodded.

"It was just a local thing. A short story contest sponsored by the *Richmond Times and News.*"

Zachery's eyebrows arched with interest. "What was your story about?"

"An accident involving a drunk driver."

"A story you made up?"

"Not exactly. I got the idea from . . ." Scott looked at his parents, as his expression changed. "My sister was in an accident."

Zachery's expression changed to one of concern.

Ellen continued for her son when he didn't explain. "Scott has a sister named Jenny. She was hurt in an accident. She's in a coma."

"I'm sorry," Zachery spoke softly. "Is she in a hospital?"

Ellen's eyes turned moist. "No. The doctors couldn't do anything else for her, so they let us bring her home."

"How long has she been this way?"

"A year."

"Today is the anniversary of the accident, Zachery," Max added, suddenly looking vulnerable.

"That must have been hard happening at Christmas time."

"We didn't celebrate Christmas last year," Max grimaced.

"Do you mind if I ask what happened?"

Ellen's voice became noticeably strained as she explained. "A drunk driver hit Jenny while she was riding her bicycle in our neighborhood. When she was thrown from her bike, she struck her head. She's been in a coma ever since."

"Did she suffer any other injuries?"

"Miraculously, no. To see her you would never even guess she was in a coma. To us, she always appears to be sleeping, doesn't she, Max?"

Max nodded.

"What do the doctors say?"

"They aren't too encouraging. They don't have any answers, except to say every case is different. They say she could stay in a coma the rest of her life, or she could just wake up one day."

Zachery toyed with his spoon, then looked at the Reids. "What do you think?"

Ellen glanced at her husband. "We were optimistic at first. Lately . . . well, it's been discouraging."

Max agreed. "It's been a long year."

"Was the driver hurt?"

"No. After hitting Jenny, he swerved and hit a tree, but he wasn't even scratched. Scott was riding his bike behind her and saw the whole thing."

"It should have been me who was hit instead," Scott mumbled the words into his plate.

The bitter tone in Scott's voice caused the conversation to go silent. Ellen reached over and touched her son's arm. "Don't say that, Scott. There was nothing you could have done."

"Son, you can't keep blaming yourself," Max added, giving Ellen a look of frustration.

Scott continued to stare down in silence.

Max turned to their guest, his voice harsh. "I don't understand why it's the drunk drivers who always walk away from an accident. Why aren't they ever hurt?"

"But they are."

"What do you mean?"

"What happened to the driver who hit your daughter?"

"He wasn't even scratched."

"I mean after the accident. Was he punished?"

"He went to prison where he belongs, although—if you can believe it—he received only a six month sentence, and then only after months of delays in court. A few lousy months in jail for ruining our child's life!" Max spit out his words.

Zachery toyed with his silverware. "Have you wondered how all this may have affected *his* life?"

"Miserably, I hope," Max replied.

"Apparently the man had personal problems," Ellen added compassionately. "I remember from the trial he had just lost his job before the accident. He talked about having a family to take care of too, as I recall."

"We all have personal problems," Max said, pushing his plate away in disgust. "That doesn't give any of us the right to get drunk and run over children."

"Have you talked with this man since the accident?"

The Reids stared at their guest. "What would we say?" Ellen asked finally.

"Like it or not, you became personally connected with him because of the accident and what he did to your daughter. I doubt that his going to jail has removed his guilt any more than it could resolve your feelings about what happened. That requires something on your part."

"Like what?" Max asked warily.

Zachery looked at each of them. "An act of forgiveness."

At the words, the room became uncomfortably quiet. No one knew how to respond to the pointed remark. Finally, Ellen decided to break the awkward silence.

"I guess if everyone is finished, why don't I serve dessert in the living room so we can enjoy the Christmas tree?" She began gathering the plates. "Scott, if you will help me, your father can take Zachery and go get a fire going.

"Max, I'll bet Zachery would enjoy hearing about the recent merger your company made." She was sending a message with her eyes for him to relax and entertain their guest. "Max worked hard putting the deal together, Zachery," she said proudly.

"I'd like to hear all about it," Zachery smiled politely. It seemed he had not noticed the awkwardness of a moment ago.

Ellen breathed a sigh of relief as she pushed the swinging door into the kitchen. Scott followed with a load of dishes. Then, while deep in thought, he watched his mother cut her homemade apple pie.

"Mom?"

"Yes?"

"What's the name of the man who hit Jenny?"

"Jake Fincastle."

"Yeah, that's it. We never have talked much about him, have we?"

"No."

"I guess we never thought about how the accident affected him either, did we?"

"I guess not." Ellen tried to focus her attention on dessert. "Would you get me the vanilla ice cream, Son?"

Scott pulled the carton from the freezer and set it on the counter. "How come?"

"I don't know. I guess we were angry about the senseless pain he had caused. It was just better not to discuss him."

She scooped ice cream beside each slice. "Besides, it was an irresponsible act, and he had to pay his debt to society."

Scott flipped one of the table knives into the air, caught it by the handle, and flipped it up again. It was a habit he had that helped him think. "I didn't realize until tonight how much Dad has hated Jake Fincastle."

Ellen looked at her son with surprise. "I don't think your father *hates* him."

"Well, I have."

"If you have, it's because of what you've been through. A tragedy like what happened to Jenny causes bitter feelings."

"So you've felt it too."

"Of course." Ellen walked over to the sink.

"Ever since the accident, there's been a gloom over our house. Haven't you felt it, Mom?"

Ellen stopped washing her hands and turned to look at her son. "What do you expect? Your sister is still in a coma in the other room."

"I know, but I think Zachery was right."

"What do you mean?" Ellen started to feel flustered again.

"About needing to forgive Mr. Fincastle."

Ellen was quiet a moment. "Perhaps he was."

"How do we do that?" asked Scott.

Ellen shrugged, "We could pray for Mr. Fincastle."

Scott wasn't satisfied, so he decided to say what he was really feeling. "I think we should visit him."

"You mean in prison?"

"Sure, why not?"

"What would we say to him?"

"The truth. Tell him how we've felt. Say we're sorry for what happened."

Ellen walked back to the island counter where her son was standing. She had to reach up to take his face in her hands. At sixteen, he was already half a head taller. She studied his sincere face, then let out a hearty laugh. "Scott, sometimes I don't know where we got you."

"So what do you think, Mom?"

"I guess it would be okay with me."

"Do you think Dad will go along with the idea?"

Ellen smiled at her son. "Let's take dessert to the living room and find out."

IV

Later that night, after everyone had gone to bed, the Reid's guest quietly slipped downstairs. A night light was on in the family room that now served as Jenny's bedroom. The warm glow illuminated a beautiful little girl lying in bed, her porcelain skin glowing in the dim light. Long curls fell across covers tucked snugly under her arms. For a long while he stood next to the bed and watched her. Then he took her hand and, bending close, whispered into her ear. Finally, he straightened up, gently stroked her hair, then quietly retreated back upstairs.

V

*T*he next morning Ellen was up earlier than usual. She thought about the night before as she tidied up Jenny's room. During dessert, she and Scott had broached the idea of visiting Jake Fincastle. At first Max had vehemently fought the idea. But he had finally relented, after some persuasion from Scott, and agreed to drive out to the prison after church today.

Ellen sighed and fluffed a pillow. She was tired from wrestling with her emotions all night. Now she wasn't so sure she could talk with the man who had hurt her Jenny. She held the pillow and gazed at her daughter lying there helpless. It was like she lay in some permanent state of living death. Sometimes she was reminded of Snow White, except this was no fairy tale. "If only Jenny were already recovered and things were back to normal," she sighed quietly. "It would be easier to face him today."

Last night she had admitted, for the first time since the accident, that a sinister cancer had crept into their home. Zachery had been right. A bitterness was slowly consuming them. *Well,* she thought, as she gave the pillow a determined fluff, *if visiting Jake Fincastle will help us get free from this bitterness, I'm willing!*

She was turning Jenny to face the morning light filtering through the windows, when a knock at the door startled her. "Good morning," the voice said quietly.

It was Zachery. Ellen felt a smile crease her face and her spirits suddenly lift. "Come in," she said, motioning to him. She noticed his clothes from last night still looked pressed.

"How is Jenny doing this morning?" he asked cheerily.

"She's fine."

Zachery moved next to the bed and stroked Jenny's hair. "I hope you don't mind that I came back downstairs to visit with her last night after everyone was asleep."

"Oh?" Ellen asked, surprised.

"I wanted to tell her about our conversation during dessert. Do you believe she can hear when you talk to her?"

"I'm not sure. The doctor told us that comatose patients can respond to a familiar voice, sometimes even familiar music. We make sure to talk to her and read to her everyday, just in case. Why? Did you think she heard you?"

"It seemed so."

Ellen picked up the brush off the night table and began fixing her daughter's hair. "I wish you could have met her before . . ." She bit her lip to hold back her emotions. "She was the most beautiful child."

"I can see that. You know, Ellen, I've seen many tragedies like yours."

"You have?"

"Unfortunately, yes." Zachery walked over to the window and looked out reflectively. "In my line of work I often visit hospitals."

For a fleeting second, Ellen thought she saw an aura glowing around him before she realized it was the light coming through the window and surrounding his silhouette. The illusion made for a strange effect.

"What I have found to be most important is how we handle our circumstances. You have a special opportunity to experience what I'm talking about today."

Ellen stopped and watched him. "You mean our visit to Jake Fincastle?"

Zachery nodded and turned to face her. "How do you feel about the decision all of you made last night?"

Ellen sighed as she braided Jenny's hair. "I had a rough night of it. In my heart I know what we're doing is right, but my head isn't so sure."

"That sounds normal enough. Just think how nervous Jake Fincastle is going to be seeing all of you arrive," Zachery added, smiling.

Ellen looked up. "You've got a point. I didn't even think about that."

There! She was finished with Jenny's hair. Now it was time to fix breakfast. "How do buckwheat pancakes and sausage sound for breakfast?"

"They sound great. Even after all the good cooking last night, I have to admit I'm famished."

"That's because you were outside all day yesterday. Come talk to me in the kitchen, while I make up a double batch."

Zachery hesitated. "I'm curious about Jenny? How does she eat?"

"We spoon feed her. That's one reason the doctors let her come home. She doesn't require tube feeding or a respirator like many comatose patients."

"It's amazing she can be in a coma and eat."

"I know. They say it's a reflexive action to swallow. Anyway, I would normally feed her in the morning, but her nurse, Daisy, will be coming in shortly. Daisy feeds and sponge bathes her for me on Sunday."

"So you have outside help?"

"Yes. Daisy comes in several times a week so I can go shopping for food, go to church, that sort of thing. She's been a godsend."

As Zachery followed Ellen into the kitchen, he asked, "Where are the menfolk? I haven't seen them this morning."

"Max is preparing the Sunday school lesson. He and I teach the junior high Sunday school class. Scott is outside playing with Beauchamps."

"That's quite a dog Scott has," Zachery laughed. "He tried to carry my bag inside for me last night."

"We got Beauchamps for Scott's tenth birthday. Those two are inseparable." She pointed to the fresh brewed pot. "Coffee?"

"Please." Zachery took the mug and found a seat at the kitchen table while Ellen started the sausage.

"You and Max have a mighty fine boy. I was impressed with him right from the start yesterday. He's a hard worker too."

"Thank you. The manager at Food-Krops always gives him a good report." Ellen paused as she turned the sausage, then continued. "Sometimes I think this ordeal has been hardest on him."

"I noticed last night. Why does he feel so guilty about what happened?"

"Because he was there that day. You see, Scott has always been a responsible big brother. The afternoon of the accident he was teaching Jenny to ride her bike without training wheels. He blames himself for taking her onto a busy street.

"He was really bad off the first few weeks after the accident, when Jenny was in intensive care. He didn't eat, he couldn't function at school, yet he wouldn't talk about it. We finally sent him to a therapist, which helped some.

"But, even after a year, he's still dealing with it. We find ourselves having to prod him to get involved in extracurricular activities which he always loved doing before, like being in the church play. Although," Ellen paused, "he did initiate entering the newspaper's writing contest on his own."

Zachery pondered a minute. "Writing the story was a safe way to deal with his feelings, I suspect."

Ellen nodded as she reached for the buckwheat flour. "Unfortunately, in the story it is the irresponsible action of the main character, a teenage boy Scott's age, which causes an accident. It was well written, but left Max and me feeling bad for Scott. It was obvious that he had made himself the story's main character.

"Countless times we have told him there was nothing he could have done to stop a drunk driver from running off the road and hitting his sister." Ellen slumped against the counter. She felt tired. "Last night was the first time he ever talked freely about the accident. I know that's why Max finally agreed to visit Jake Fincastle. He did it for Scott."

"I figured as much," Zachery replied, sipping his coffee thoughtfully. "You realize Scott may find it easier to forgive this man, Jake Fincastle, than himself?"

"Well, I don't know what else we can try to do." Ellen gave a look of helplessness, then turned to face the counter.

"Just let today run its course," Zachery replied quietly.

But Ellen didn't hear. She had already started the mixer.

After a hearty breakfast, the Reids and Zachery left for church, leaving Jenny with Daisy. After church that afternoon, they made the drive to the correctional prison located in outlying Goochland County. Everyone was quiet during the drive as an uneasiness about meeting with Jake Fincastle settled over them.

Driving up the winding hill to the compound, Max instructed everyone to wait in the van while he walked ahead to okay their visit. A call was made from the guardhouse, and the sergeant in charge reported to the gate where Max waited. The female sergeant listened politely as he explained the purpose of his family's visit. Then she excused herself to make a call, saying the warden's permission was needed.

When she returned, she was nodding. "Warden said okay. Usually visitors have to be approved ahead of time. No exceptions." She shrugged. "You must have caught him in the Christmas spirit. Of course, the inmate will have to agree to see you."

Max nodded that he understood.

"Wave your family to come over. We'll start getting you checked inside."

The sergeant escorted them through a caged breezeway and into a chapel which doubled as the prison's visiting area. There they were given the standard search required of all visitors then told to wait while Jake Fincastle was notified.

"I didn't know we were going to be searched," Scott whispered uneasily, not wanting the guard standing on the other side of the chain linked cage to hear.

"It wouldn't be a fun place to be, would it?" his father asked.

Scott shook his head.

"And this is only a medium security facility. Hardened criminals go to much worse prisons."

There was some movement at the front of the chapel. They immediately recognized Jake Fincastle when he entered the room. They remembered him being a slight man. Now, if anything, he was even thinner than at the trial. That he had lived a hard life was obvious. Deep lines creased his face like old shoe leather. His walk was stiff and his posture bent as if he were carrying a heavy tool box.

For a moment they stared awkwardly at one another, then Max cleared his throat and spoke. "Jake, I think you recognize my family and me. I'm Max Reid, this is my wife Ellen and our son Scott. And this is our friend Zachery."

Zachery, who was standing off from the group, nodded at Jake with a smile.

Jake awkwardly nodded at everyone. From his expression it was clear he didn't know how to respond.

Max looked at Ellen and Scott before he continued. "The reason we've come here today is to tell you that we're sorry for what happened and to let you know that we want to put the accident behind us."

Jake stared at them without speaking.

Max glanced at Zachery, then continued, "And to say how we regret that this tragedy has ruined your life too."

At these words, Jake suddenly began to tremble. His shoulders heaved and his emotions cracked. Slumping in a chair, he buried his face in his hands and began weeping.

The Reids waited, uncertain of what else to do. Scott placed his arm around his mother, as she dabbed her eyes with a tissue.

Finally, when Jake could compose himself enough to speak, he raised his head. "I'm sorry," he sniffled and wiped his eyes. "Excuse me a minute."

The Reids sat quietly and waited while Jake went off into a corner of the visiting area to compose himself. Scott looked back at Zachery who gave him a reassuring nod.

After a few minutes, Jake returned, sat upright in the chair, and faced them, his eyes still red. "I guess I lost it there. I . . . I don't know what to say. I figured you must hate me for what happened."

"We did, until our friend here opened our eyes." Max pointed to Zachery. "He showed us we had become bitter since the accident. I don't think we were even aware of it, except we knew something wasn't right." Max looked at his wife and son who nodded their agreement. "That's why we've come here today, Jake. We want to get things right with you, and with ourselves."

Jake stammered out his reply, "I've been torn up inside ever since the accident. Your daughter . . . ? Is she . . . ? How is she?"

"Jenny's still in a coma," Ellen said, speaking for the first time.

"I pray for her everyday. God knows if I had it to do all over again, I would rather have killed myself than hurt your little girl."

"We know," she said softly, "we can see it written on your face."

"Soon after I arrived here a chaplain explained how I could have forgiveness for what I done. I've been praying for your daughter everyday since. I wanted to write and ask about her, but I didn't have the nerve."

Jake's voice cracked with emotion. "If I could only relive that day . . . I had just been laid off my job of eleven years. The pressure of finding new work and taking care of my family in the meantime was just too much. Christmas was on me too. I didn't have no money to buy presents, so I done the cowardly thing and went to a bar to forget my problems. You know the rest . . ."

Jake hung his head a moment before he continued. "I never could have dreamed you would come see me, that I would have the chance to tell you in person how sorry I am." He looked at the Reids, his face sincere. "Will you forgive me for what I done to you and your daughter?"

The Reids quickly looked at one another, then back at Jake and answered, "Yes."

Jake's countenance lightened for the first time. "I told God I would do anything—anything, if He would make your daughter well."

"He hears those kinds of prayers," Ellen reached over and patted Jake's arm.

For a moment they were all quiet, then Max broke the silence. "When do you get out?"

"Later in January."

"What are your plans?"

"Get a job, and get to know my family again. My wife, Shannon, and our three children have had it rough this past year. I don't know how she has kept everything together."

"What kind of work do you do?"

"Plant work. I hope I can find a company that's hiring."

"How's your family faring this holiday?" Ellen asked.

Jake looked away. "They're making it, I guess." His eyes revealed differently. "In addition to her full-time job, Shannon's taken a part-time job at Wal-Mart for the holidays. That should bring in a little extra money for Christmas. Her mother tries to help some too."

Ellen drew her chair closer. "Jake, we would like to do something for your family for Christmas. Perhaps Shannon and the kids could use a Christmas meal? Would you mind if I called and offered?"

"You don't have to do that."

"But I want to."

"Mom," Scott spoke up, "perhaps Mr. Fincastle's family would like to come to the Christmas play tonight."

"That's a good idea, Scott," Ellen replied, then explained. "We have a live nativity play every Christmas Eve at our church, Jake. It's quite popular. We would love to take your family as our guests—if you think they would enjoy going."

"I could call Shannon and find out." Jake hesitated. "She ain't got no car, though."

"That's all right, we can pick your family up." Ellen looked at Max who nodded his head in agreement.

"Give me a minute and I'll call her."

The Reids gave each other satisfied looks as Jake left the room. Zachery spoke first. "Are you pleased with how it's going?"

They nodded.

"I plan to talk with my home office. Perhaps we can help Jake's family."

"That would be wonderful, Zachery!" Ellen exclaimed.

"Do you think Food-Krop's might want to help too?" Max asked his son.

Scott perked up. "Yeah, I'll bet they would! They're always helping people in the community."

While they continued to wait for Jake, they began discussing different ways the Fincastle family could be helped. When Jake returned, he was smiling. "I got hold of Shannon, and she said yes! The kids have been begging her to do something special for Christmas."

"Wonderful!" Ellen said excitedly. "You told her we would be picking her up?"

Jake nodded. "I got to warn you though, at first she was real hesitant. It might take her a while to warm up."

"We understand."

"I told Shannon you would be calling her this afternoon." Ellen nodded and quickly wrote down the address and phone number.

Max decided to make the offer he was thinking over. "We'd like to come visit you again before you get out, Jake."

Jake seemed overwhelmed. "I never met any people like you folks. One day I hope to tell your daughter, face-to-face, how sorry I am for what happened."

"She would appreciate that, Jake," Ellen replied softly.

The Reids took a few minutes to ask Jake about his family, then prepared to go. Jake turned to Zachery, who was still standing a polite distance away, and gave him a curious look. "I'd like to shake your hand. I know you done something wonderful getting these fine people here today."

Zachery took his hand and squeezed it. "Things are going to get better for you, Jake."

"I'm counting on it. They ain't never gone too good before."

"That's true," Zachery nodded in agreement, "but you're on the right track now."

VI

$\mathscr{I}$t was six o'clock when the Reids crossed the James River on their way to pick up the Fincastle family. After leaving Jake, they had returned home so Ellen could call Shannon and put together a meal for the Fincastles, using some of the food she had prepared for their own Christmas dinner. Meanwhile, Max had dropped Scott off at church for his final dress rehearsal. At the last minute, Zachery had decided to stay with Scott at church. Now, riding alone in the car, it was Max and Ellen's first chance to discuss the afternoon.

"I was proud of you today," Ellen said, leaning over and squeezing her husband's hand. Max smiled as he strained to look over the bridge railing to catch a glimpse of the river, but it was too dark to see anything. Ellen continued, "The way you spoke to Jake for all of us touched me."

"I have to admit I didn't know how I was going to react beforehand. But when he walked into the room, and I saw he was a broken man, I knew I couldn't hate him."

"He'll never forget what you did."

Max sighed. "I don't know about you, but I feel like a big sack has been lifted off my back."

"Zachery was right about what he said last night, wasn't he?"

"Yes, I have to admit he was." Max glanced over at his wife. "What do you think about him?"

"What do you mean?" Ellen made a questioning look.

"I mean his showing up on the anniversary of the accident, and now this whole thing today."

Ellen was silent a moment. "Maybe he was supposed to . . . I don't know what to think," she shrugged.

Max continued to stare through the windshield. "I just wish I could put it together where I know him from. It sure would make me feel better." He noticed an exit sign up ahead. "Is this it?"

"Yes." Ellen turned on her reading light and quickly rechecked the directions. "Take a left at the bottom of the ramp."

"How did Shannon sound about coming?" Max asked, making the turn.

"Reserved, like Jake said. But, in all fairness, she wasn't there today."

As they followed the directions into a modest neighborhood, Max and Ellen began to mentally prepare to meet Jake's family. Max located the house number and pulled off the street in front of a bungalow. They both smiled when they noticed little faces peeking out the front window.

A demure woman greeted them at the door and welcomed them inside. It was Shannon. "Come over here where you can meet Mr. and Mrs. Reid," she motioned to her children. She gave the Reids a nervous smile. "They've been asking all sorts of questions about the Christmas play."

A gangly boy, tall for his age, stepped forward. "This is Gary, our oldest. He's twelve." Gary offered a limp handshake and a mumble, then backed away, his eyes staying locked on the floor. It was obvious he was uncomfortable.

Shannon offered the Reids an embarrassed shrug, then moved to the next child. "This is Sherrie, she's seven." A pretty girl with big eyes offered a shy hello.

Ellen noticed the dainty dress and red bow holding back her long brown hair. "You look very pretty tonight," she said, leaning over and giving the girl a wide smile. The girl beamed at the compliment.

Shannon looked down at the tot hiding behind her skirt. He had not taken his eyes off the Reids the whole time. "This is my youngest. We call him *Little* Jake. He's three." Uncertain eyes stared up at them.

Max pulled something out of his coat pocket and knelt down to Little Jake's level. "Do you like candy canes?" he asked, holding out the peppermint. The little boy's eyes grew round with delight as he grabbed for the candy.

The child's response brought a laugh from the adults that helped relieve some of the tension. "You just made a friend for life," Shannon smiled at Max.

"That's what I wanted," Max replied, mussing the little boy's hair, then turned to offer the two older children candy canes. Sherrie accepted with a polite thank you, while Gary shook his head no.

"Let's hurry and get our coats on, children," Shannon urged them.

Ellen watched as Shannon helped her children with their coats. She was a thin woman. Probably in her mid-thirties, Ellen guessed. Her large brown eyes held a sadness that disclosed a life of difficulty. Still, her face was attractive. Like her daughter, she had long, brown hair which she pulled back in a ponytail that hung halfway down her back. Ellen noticed she was wearing a summer dress that looked barely warm enough for inside the drafty house, much less for braving the outdoors.

The surroundings were meager too, with the only sitting

furniture in the living room being a dilapidated sofa and two vinyl chairs with rips that revealed yellow stuffing. A worn carpet remnant covered part of the painted floor. Displayed on an old coffee table was a small, artificial Christmas tree with tiny red balls and a string of blinking colored lights. Ellen counted three small presents beneath the tree and felt a stab of pity as she realized the family's situation.

Shannon noticed her looking around and apologized for the furnishings. "A few months ago I had to sell our furniture in the *Trading Gazette*. I found these things at the flea market."

"You don't need to apologize," Ellen replied reassuringly. "You've had a lot of responsibility on you this past year. Jake really hates what you've been going through. He told us so."

"You do what you have to do," Shannon shrugged. The woman allowed her eyes to make contact with Ellen for the first time. "I don't know how you could come here," she whispered.

Ellen reached over and touched Shannon's arm. "It may be hard to understand when I say this, but we're grateful to be here."

"Well, whatever happened today must have been special, because it sure affected Jake. I could tell by his voice on the phone."

Ellen looked over at Max and smiled. "It was."

Giving the cap on Little Jake's head a final pull, Shannon announced that she and the children were ready.

"Then let's go!" Max exclaimed and offered his arms to the tot.

"I'll take you, Little Jake," Gary intercepted the offer and grabbed his brother's hand. Max caught his wife's eye and made an expression that asked, *What's his problem?*

VII

The Reid's mini-van had three rows of seats. The boys climbed on the bench in the very back, while Shannon and Sherrie sat on the middle seat behind the Reids. On the way to church, Max and Ellen made conversation with the children, asking about their school activities and friends. Twenty minutes later they pulled into the church's already crowded parking lot, then hurried to find Zachery who was waiting for them in the vestibule.

Before the Reids could make introductions, Zachery spoke to the children.

"How did you know their names?" Shannon asked him with bewilderment.

Zachery began bouncing Little Jake, who had already climbed into his arms. "Oh, I must have heard their father mention their names this afternoon."

Max, who was looking through the large double doors leading into the sanctuary, motioned for everyone. "Come on! We'd better find some seats."

"Not to worry," Zachery said, waving everyone to follow him. "I saved us a pew."

As they filed into their pew, Mrs. Brigglesworth saw them and hurried over. "Hello, you two!" she said to Max and Ellen, flashing her trademark smile and giving them each a hug.

She was wearing a huge Christmas tree brooch on her coat lapel, with red and green rhinestones that substituted for tree ornaments. "You two must be so excited," she fluttered. "Scott told me all about his part when I saw him at the grocery store yesterday. I can't wait to see him riding that camel!" Mrs. B. noticed Shannon and the children for the first time. "You brought guests, I see."

Ellen made the introductions. When she got to Zachery, Mrs. B. suddenly became flustered. Max nudged Ellen, as they watched Mrs. B. respond like a nervous debutante at a cotillion. She was obviously taken with their handsome guest.

Zachery offered a polite hello, then turned his attention back to playing with Little Jake.

Mrs. B. sniffed at Zachery's seeming offhandedness then, without missing a beat, turned to Ellen. "Guess who's coming to see me tomorrow?" Not waiting for an answer, she gushed on in her mile-a-minute style, "My son Robby and his family. I'm so excited! I haven't seen them for six months! They live in Delaware now, you know."

"I remember," Ellen nodded. "That's wonderful." She was glad Mrs. B. was having family come for the holidays, especially since this was her first Christmas alone. Her husband, Fred, had passed away earlier in the year.

The lights blinked. It was the signal for everyone to take their seats. The play was about to begin. Mrs. B. wished everyone a Merry Christmas and whisked off to her seat. The children, who had been briefed about Scott's role riding the camel, now fidgeted with excitement as the lights dimmed.

Max looked over at Gary with a smile. Thinking that no one was watching, even he had let his guard down.

The spot light focused on the minister as he began reading the Christmas Story from the Bible. The first scene opened with the angel Gabriel appearing to Zechariah and foretelling the birth of John the Baptist. As the passage was read, the scene was acted out.

The scene arrived with the shepherds on the hillside outside of Bethlehem watching their flocks. Suddenly, angels dressed in cascading white garments descended from hidden places in the ceiling. Max nudged his wife. The Reids watched with delight as the Fincastle children's mouths dropped open, and their eyes grew round in wonder. Suspended between floor and ceiling by nearly invisible wires, the angels announced the arrival of the Christ Child to the shepherds. Even Zachery's face radiated with pleasure at the spectacle which looked very real.

Once again the sanctuary darkened as the scene changed. "It's almost time for Scott," Ellen excitedly passed the word down the pew.

As the caravan of wise men made its way into the church, the children spontaneously leaped to their feet to get a better look. The first two wise men were seated in palanquins, which moved down the aisle in exaggerated pomp, the poles of their carriages resting on the shoulders of foot servants. Following behind, Scott was riding the camel. Squeals of delight sounded throughout the church as the strange creature plodded down the aisle.

The Reids watched proudly as Scott passed by. He was dressed in a colored tapestry robe, which Ellen had made, along with a glittering gold turban. Max chuckled as he watched his son rocking back and forth. "He's going to need a chiropractor after tonight," he whispered to Ellen.

"Just hope that animal behaves," Ellen elbowed him nervously. Perched atop the animal's huge hump, Scott appeared to his mother to be ten feet up in the air. At the front, Scott dismounted and joined the other wise men as they presented their gifts to the Christ Child.

For the final act, Santa Claus appeared on stage. Approaching the Christ Child, he knelt reverently alongside the shepherds and wise men.

With the play over, it was time for the "Lighting of the Candles." Everyone had received a candle before the play began, which they now lit by passing the flame from one candle to the next, until the whole sanctuary was filled with hundreds of lights. Raising their candles toward the ceiling, the congregation sang *Silent Night* a cappella.

Following the service, an announcement was made that Santa Claus had presents down front for all the children. The Fincastle children pulled at their mother excitedly. "Can we go too?" they asked.

Shannon looked at Ellen. "Of course you can," Ellen smiled.

Little Jake and Sherrie each grabbed a hand and tugged Zachery down to the front, while Gary followed awkwardly behind.

Shannon turned to Ellen. "The play was wonderful! I like the way Santa came in and knelt at the end."

"It's our way of saying to the children that Santa would have paid homage too, had he been there in Bethlehem that first night."

"I never saw the Christmas story so real. I can't wait to tell Jake about it."

"Well, we hope he will come next year."

"He told me we're going to start attending church when he gets out. I hope he means it."

"I think you are going to find a lot of things different, Shannon," Ellen said reassuringly.

As the women talked, Max watched the children work their way up to Santa, who had a couple of young people dressed as elves helping him pass out gifts.

Shannon's voice faltered as she spoke. "I've been wanting to ask how your daughter is doing. Jake said she's still in a coma." The guilt, which Ellen had seen in Shannon's eyes earlier, had returned.

"Unfortunately, she's still the same."

"I can't imagine how you could be so kind after what has happened. I don't think I could."

Ellen reached for Max's hand with a smile. "Actually, seeing Jake today helped us resolve some things."

"I have to admit, I've noticed a change in Jake over the last several months."

"In what way?" Max asked.

"He talks about mending his old ways, for one thing. That's a big change." Shannon was thoughtful a moment. "You know, for the first time since all this has happened, I'm actually looking forward to Jake coming home so we can start over."

As the adults were talking, Scott entered the sanctuary. Seeing his folks, he waved and walked over. He had already changed back into his street clothes. "How did you like the play?" he asked.

"It was wonderful!" they exclaimed.

"Weren't you scared up on that camel?" Shannon asked.

"Oh, it was nothing," Scott answered modestly, and explained to Shannon how docile Penelope was.

Just then the children came running back up the aisle with Zachery in tow. Each was holding a little package. "Look what we got!" they shouted in chorus.

"Aren't you going to open them?" Shannon asked.

"We're going to wait so we can have more presents under the tree," Gary spoke for his brother and sister.

"Do you recognize him?" Shannon pointed to Scott.

"Yeah!" Gary said, looking up at the older boy with awe in his eyes. "He was on the camel."

Max tossed Scott the keys. "Why don't you take Gary, and you two go warm up the van?"

"Want to?" Scott asked the younger boy.

"Sure!" As the two of them left, Gary was wearing a big smile. He looked proud to be included with the older boy.

Max turned to the rest of them with a mischievous look. "Need I remind everyone it's Christmas Eve? If Santa comes and we're not home, he may go on to the next house."

The children didn't need any more prompting to begin moving toward the parking lot.

VIII

On the way back to the Fincastle's home, Ellen sat next to Shannon so they could talk. "I have some dishes of food in the back I thought you could use for tomorrow's meal."

"You people are too much!" Shannon shook her head with emotion. "But we sure can use it."

"Do you get out to the correctional center to see Jake much?" Max asked, turning around to face Shannon from where he was sitting in the front passenger seat.

"Not often. I don't have a car, and it's hard to catch a ride. My mother has taken me a couple of times, but she works a lot too."

"Would you like to visit during the holidays?"

"Of course, but I don't know how . . ."

"We would take you. We promised Jake today we'd come visit."

"That would be wonderful!"

Sherrie perked up upon hearing them talk about her father. "Mommy, are we going to see Daddy?"

"Yes, I hope so."

"Oh, goodie!"

"How about it, Gary?" Shannon turned to her son, who was sitting beside Zachery on the last seat.

"I don't want to go," he mumbled. As the excitement of the play had worn off, Gary had regained his earlier, sullen mood.

"Gary has refused to visit his father in prison," Shannon whispered to the Reids.

Max looked back to see Gary ignoring his mother and looking out the side window. Now he understood the source of the boy's anger. He was resentful of his father.

Zachery leaned over and whispered something into the boy's ear. Gary shook his head defiantly. After a few minutes back and forth, tears began to run down the boy's cheeks. Finally he looked up at Zachery and nodded.

"Go ahead and tell her then," Zachery prodded him gently.

"Tell me what?" Shannon turned around in her seat to look at them.

"Okay, I'll go," Gary mumbled.

"To see your father?"

The boy nodded.

Shannon gave Zachery a look of amazement. "What did you say to him?"

Zachery smiled with a shrug. "Oh, just that everything was going to be all right."

Shannon reached back and squeezed Zachery's hand. "Thank you."

"Let me tell you what I want for Christmas," said Sherrie, turning around to face her new friend.

"That's all I need now," Shannon moaned. "Honey, I told you Santa may not be able to visit us this Christmas. Now, you're going to get your little brother all excited."

"Let the children have fun. It's Christmas Eve," Zachery

gently prodded Shannon. Addressing her anxious eyes, he said to Sherrie, "Tell me what you want for Christmas."

Shannon raised her hands in resignation as Sherrie and little Jake launched into their want lists. They were still reeling off the names of games, dolls, and toy cars when Scott pulled the van up in front of the Fincastle house.

"I wonder what that could be?" Shannon asked, noticing two large bags on the front porch.

The kids didn't wait for the adults as they darted out of the van and ran to the porch to see. Suddenly, they were shouting excitedly.

"What is it?" Shannon called out.

Gary hoisted a bag. "They're full of presents, Mom!"

"What?" Shannon ran down the sidewalk to see for herself. Looking at all the presents, her mouth fell open. "How in the world?" She pointed to the bags with a look of bewilderment, as the Reids reached the porch. "Will you look at this?"

"Let's take them inside and see who they're for," Zachery prodded with a hint of amusement.

"Something strange is going on," Shannon shook her head, staring at Max and Ellen.

The Reids looked just as bewildered as they filed up the steps and into the house. Max and Scott quickly deposited the dishes of food in the kitchen which Ellen had prepared and joined the activity in the living room. The children were rummaging wildly through the bags, trying to figure out which presents were their own.

"Hey, this one's got my name on it!" Gary said excitedly. He held up a wrapped present. It was a square box with bulging sides. "It feels like a basketball, Mom! Zachery, you were right!"

"What was Zachery right about?" Shannon asked.

"That this Christmas would be different!" Gary gave Zachery an admiring gaze.

"Santa Claus must have come while we were at church!" Sherrie announced, holding up a long present with her name on it.

"He came to see me too!" Little Jake made a struggling attempt to lift a gift half as big as himself. The comical scene made everyone laugh.

Shannon gave her daughter a nod. "I guess Santa did come after all." Turning to the Reids, she whispered, "And you didn't have anything to do with this?"

Max and Ellen shook their heads emphatically. "No, honest."

"I don't understand." Tears welled up in Shannon's eyes. "I've never had anything like this happen before."

Noticing Scott kneeling on the floor, the adults watched as he helped the children guess the contents of their presents.

"Scott, you're going to have to apply as Santa's helper at church next year," his father kidded good-naturedly.

Scott's smile said it all. He was enjoying the moment.

Finally, after all the gifts were sorted by child, the Reids began to make their way to the door. It was time to leave so the children could get to bed.

"Kids," their mother leaned close and whispered, "don't forget to tell Scott how much you enjoyed the play, and thank the Reids for inviting us."

The children cheered Scott until he blushed. Wanting to take the attention off himself, he said to Gary, "Sounds like you enjoy playing basketball."

"Yeah."

"Maybe you would like to go to the gym sometime."

"Sure," Gary grinned.

Out on the porch, Max looked at the sky. "I wouldn't be surprised to see a white Christmas come morning." His forecast brought a fresh round of claps and squeals from the children.

"Remember what we agreed," Zachery reminded Gary with a hand on his shoulder.

Gary looked up at Zachery with a boy's affection for a grandfather. "I won't forget."

Max and Ellen gave each other satisfied looks over the change in the boy's attitude.

"I'll be saying a special prayer for Jenny," Shannon promised quietly, as the two women said good-bye. They agreed to talk later about visiting Jake.

The children were still dancing with excitement on their porch as the Reids drove out of sight.

IX

*W*hen they arrived home, Ellen went straight to her daughter's room. She found Daisy sitting in the rocking chair reading a Christmas story out loud to Jenny.

"How was the play?" the matronly nurse looked up.

"Wonderful. It was the best production ever." Ellen felt herself brimming with pride. "Scott was a hit riding the camel."

"I wish I could have seen him sitting on top of that beast. What a sight for sore eyes that must have been!" Saying that, Daisy let out one of her belly laughs that Ellen always enjoyed hearing. "How about the family, did they have a good time?"

Sitting down on the edge of the bed, Ellen shared the details of the evening. When she came to the part about the bags of presents on the porch, Daisy's eyes grew round. "You don't know where the presents came from?" Ellen shook her head. "What about the father? Maybe he had them delivered."

Ellen explained, "He doesn't have the money. Besides, he

would have told Shannon. She didn't have a clue. Whoever it was had to know the family, because each present had a child's name on it."

Daisy whistled. "Strange things have been going on around here too. Wait till I tell you what happened while you were gone tonight."

Ellen felt her heart leap. Instinctively she turned to check her daughter. "Is everything all right?"

"No emergencies," the nurse waved her hand. "But earlier this evening I went to the kitchen to make some tea." She leaned forward in the rocker to get closer to Ellen. "When I came back, Jenny was stirring like she was trying to wake up. Have you ever seen her do that?"

At Daisy's words, a shiver ran through Ellen like a current of electricity. She shook her head no and leaned over to study her daughter's face. Jenny looked peaceful, as usual. "Are you sure, Daisy?"

"The Lord as my witness."

"What happened next?"

"Nothing. After a few seconds she stopped." The nurse was trying hard to suppress her excitement. "For a minute, I thought she would open her eyes."

Ellen's voice rose. "What happened after that?"

"She never stirred again. I know, because I watched her all evening. Maybe we shouldn't get our hopes up too much." Daisy's demeanor had turned professional again.

"I've got to tell Max!" Ellen stood up suddenly.

"Tell me what?" asked Max. He had just entered the room.

"Honey, it's Jenny! Daisy saw her stirring tonight."

"You're kidding!" Max rushed over to his daughter. Leaning close, he gently opened her eyelids to check her pupils. The doctor had told them any change in the pupils reaction to light might be a sign she was beginning to respond.

Daisy moved next to him. "I checked them already. There's no change."

Ellen was unable to control her trembling. "Remember the doctors said this might happen, Max? Do you think she could finally be coming out of it?"

Max's face was blank. "I don't know."

"Should we call Dr. Hargrove, Daisy?"

They both looked at Daisy. She was a retired pediatric nurse with experience in these matters.

"Why don't you keep a close watch on her through Christmas and see what happens. Either way, I would call Dr. Hargrove first thing Tuesday morning. I'm sure he will want to examine her, perhaps even order a brain scan."

Max looked at Ellen, who nodded reluctantly.

The elderly nurse squeezed Ellen's hand. "This has been quite a day for all of you, hasn't it?"

Ellen nodded faintly.

"I know the two of you are exhausted."

"Except we may be too excited to sleep now," Max replied. "Come on, we need to let you get home, Daisy."

They followed Daisy to the door, where Ellen gave her a hug. "Thank you for staying all day. We know you made a sacrifice being away from your own family."

"I didn't mind at all. I think of Jenny as my daughter too." The Reids knew she meant it. "By the way, where are Scott and your guest?"

"They're outside in the garage," Max answered. "Scott is showing him our mechanic's shop."

"He came in Jenny's room and visited with me this afternoon. What an interesting man! I was telling him about the hospital in Pittsburgh, where I worked before moving to Richmond to be with my daughter and, turns out, he's been there! He knew all about the Pediatric ward and some of the doctors and nurses from when I was there. Apparently, he once visited a child there who was in critical care." Daisy smiled. "I bet you didn't know your guest this weekend was so special."

Max and Ellen exchanged looks of surprise.

"Well, let me get along. I'll stop off at the garage and wish them a Merry Christmas before I leave."

As Max opened the door for Daisy, he slipped an envelope from his coat pocket and handed it to her. "This is a special thank you for taking care of our daughter this past year. Merry Christmas!" With her emotions showing, Daisy accepted the envelope and left.

As they stood at the door watching Daisy make her way out to the garage, Max turned to Ellen. "What do you make of that? What are the odds of Zachery visiting Daisy's old hospital in Pittsburgh?"

Ellen shrugged absently. "I guess I'm not surprised with everything else happening." She was thinking more about Jenny. "Max, do you think we should tell Scott about tonight? I mean, I don't want to get his hopes up prematurely."

"He would be upset if we didn't tell him."

"You're right." She pulled her husband close. "I'm so excited. But I'm scared too. We don't know if Jenny will be okay, even if she does regain consciousness. Maybe there will be brain damage." Ellen choked out the words as she said them.

"Hold on now," Max held up his hand. "Remember, we take this one step at a time, like we have all along."

Ellen had to agree. "You're right."

They were still standing at the door looking outside when Max suddenly snapped his fingers. "Hey, we almost forgot!"

"Forgot what?"

"Our tradition of opening one present on Christmas Eve."

Every Christmas Eve the Reids gathered around the tree while each family member was allowed to select one gift to open early. The ritual made Christmas Eve fun and served to release some of the pent-up excitement.

"I *had* forgotten," Ellen laughed at herself. "This day has just been too much!"

"Don't you think we should?"

"Of course. Zachery will enjoy watching us too."

"You don't think he'll feel left out?"

"I have a present for him," Ellen smiled coyly. Max looked surprised. "Just something I had on hand. Now, if you will get a fire going and call in the men, I'll put on the hot chocolate."

"It's a deal!" Max said, heading out to the garage.

When Ellen entered the living room the men were already seated around a crackling fire. "Hot chocolate everyone!" she announced, placing the tray of steaming mugs on the coffee table. She sat down on the couch where she could keep an eye on Jenny in the next room.

As Max reached for a cup, she whispered in his ear, "Did you tell them?"

"No. I was waiting for you."

"Guess what happened tonight?" she beamed.

Zachery raised his eyebrows.

"What?" Scott asked from the floor, where he was playing with Beauchamps next to the hearth.

Ellen related to Scott and Zachery what Daisy had said. Before she could finish, Scott jumped up and ran to check on his sister. He came back into the living room, his emotions stumbling over his words as he tried to speak. "Wh . . . what happened?"

"That's everything. But isn't it wonderful?"

"It truly is," Zachery said with a peaceful smile.

"Does it mean . . . ?" Scott still couldn't say it.

"Does it mean Jenny will come out of her coma?" his father finished the sentence. "We don't know yet, Son."

"It's a good sign that she might," his mother added confidently. "Dr. Hargrove told us to expect something like this, remember?" She carried a mug of chocolate over and handed it to her son.

Scott took the mug and faced the fire. "Mrs. B. told me yesterday she had dreamed that Jenny recovered. I didn't believe her." The adults were quiet as they watched him. "Maybe it has something to do with us going to see Mr. Fincastle today."

"What do you mean, Son?" his father asked.

"I don't know, I'm just thinking."

"Well, we'd like to hear what you're thinking."

"I mean, maybe God was waiting for us to visit Jake before he could help Jenny."

"That's an interesting thought," Max pondered.

"Certainly, Jake was a changed man by the time you left today," Zachery noted.

"We all came away changed," Ellen added.

"I didn't."

Everyone looked at Scott again.

"You haven't forgiven Jake Fincastle?" his father asked, surprised.

"That's not what I mean."

Zachery balanced his cup as he leaned forward. "You mean you still feel responsible for your sister and haven't forgiven yourself, don't you, Scott?"

Scott nodded, his back still to Zachery.

Max looked at Ellen, then slid onto the ottoman beside his son. "Scott, if you don't stop blaming yourself, you'll never have any peace about this."

Tears ran down Scott's cheeks as he stared into the fire. "But it was my fault."

Max placed his arm around his son's shoulders. "No, it wasn't, Scott. What happened to Jenny would have happened even if I had been there instead of you. We have to accept that some things happen in life that are beyond our ability to control."

Scott looked at his father. "So, it really wasn't my fault?"

Max shook his head. "I've tried to tell you that, Son, for a long time."

Realizing that Max and Scott needed a few minutes of privacy, Ellen and Zachery turned toward one another to make conversation. "I've been admiring your tree ornaments, Ellen," Zachery began. "They're so unusual."

"I started collecting them when I was a little girl."

"The bells, too?"

"Those are Jenny's." Ellen walked over to the tree, lifted a bell off its branch and handed it to Zachery as she explained, "Ever since she was a baby, Jenny has loved bells. Max says she inherited it from his grandmother. We have made a tradition of giving her a bell every Christmas."

Zachery held up the shiny brass bell and admired it. "It's beautiful. Which one is this year's?" he asked, handing it back.

Ellen frowned as she took the bell and positioned it back on the branch. "We didn't get her one this Christmas."

"It's been hard, hasn't it?"

"The worst year of our lives," she smiled weakly. As Ellen looked at Zachery, she realized he was no longer a stranger to them. After the events of the past twenty-four hours, he was now their friend.

Scott and his father turned around and faced them. Scott was still wiping his eyes, as Max shot them a satisfied look and announced, "We're ready to open presents, if you two are."

Zachery looked surprised. "You open your presents on Christmas Eve?"

"Just one apiece," Ellen qualified.

"Let's open them in Jenny's room, Mom," Scott suggested.

"Good idea, Scott," Ellen said, glad to see that her son's demeanor had noticeably improved. "Pick out your present, and I'll be right back." She left the room and returned carrying a gift. "Zachery, this is to you from all of us." Ellen handed him the gift. "Careful, it's heavy."

Zachery looked delighted, then frowned. "I'm sorry I don't have a thing for any of you," he looked at them apologetically.

"Your visit with us this weekend has been present enough," Ellen hugged him affectionately.

"Mom, Dad, how about your gift?"

Ellen knew which present Scott had in mind. "Why don't you pick it out for us," she suggested. She was busy rummaging under the tree looking for Daisy's gift to Jenny. *There!* She had found it.

With gifts in hand, they moved into Jenny's bedroom and gathered around her bed. "Scott, open your sister's gift first," his mother said, handing him Daisy's present.

Scott sat on the edge of the bed, peeled the wrapping paper off, and lifted out a square of delicately stitched material. "Look, Jenny, it's a . . . ?" He unfolded the material, hoping to get a better idea of what it was he was holding.

His mother laughed. "It's a pillowcase, Scott. A beautifully brocaded pillowcase," she added, examining it closely. "Max, would you lift Jenny's head so I can put it on her pillow?"

Ellen smoothed out the pillow and placed it back beneath her daughter's head. For a moment, everyone was quiet. What Daisy had reported was fresh in their thoughts as they looked at Jenny.

"She looks as if she would wake up if you spoke too loudly," Zachery observed quietly.

As he watched his sister, Scott was tempted to try and waken her. On several occasions right after the accident, when the nurses weren't in the hospital room, he had prodded Jenny and called her name out loudly, thinking it might make her regain consciousness. He thought better of trying it now.

"You're next," his father said, breaking into his thoughts.

Scott reached for the large box from his cousins in North Carolina. Tearing off a wild pattern of Christmas paper, Scott pulled out a pair of hiking boots.

"Just what I need for next summer," Scott exclaimed. He and his father had plans for a camping trip into the Blue Ridge Mountains to hike and canoe. Scott laced up the boots and proudly stomped around the room, showing them off.

"You'll have to call your cousins first thing in the morning and thank them, Scott," his mother reminded, then turned to Zachery with a smile. "You're next."

Zachery unwrapped three jars of homemade preserves, then held one up labeled *damson*. "These look delicious."

"Something to remember your Christmas with the Reids by," Ellen smiled. "When you run out, you'll have to come back for more."

Zachery's eyes twinkled at that. "You can count on it."

"Here's yours." Scott handed his parents an envelope.

His mother opened the card and read it, while his father looked over her shoulder. She lifted out two fifty dollar bills. "What a nice gesture, Scott," she said, handing Zachery the card to read.

"That's mighty thoughtful, Son," his father patted him on the back. The card promised a weekend getaway for just the two of them while Scott helped Daisy take care of Jenny. After this past year, Scott knew they badly needed the rest.

Max picked up the Bible on the night table. "Since Jenny missed the play tonight, why don't we read the Christmas story to her. Zachery, will you do the honors?"

"What if, instead, I tell a story of that first Christmas night as I once heard it?"

Everyone liked Zachery's idea and hastily found a seat. Ellen dimmed the lights so only the Christmas tree shined into the room. Then, with the entrancing voice of a master storyteller, Zachery began by describing the village of Bethlehem and the outlying countryside of two thousand years ago. With vivid detail, he described the appearance of the angel that night to an unsuspecting group of shepherds watching their flock outside of town.

As Scott listened to Zachery describe the accompanying heavenly host, he watched the tree lights twinkle and allowed their magic to carry him back in time to that ancient night. To Scott, the shepherds had always been vague characters in an often-told story. But tonight, their story came to life.

According to Zachery's legend, one of the shepherd boys who visited the manger that Christmas night later helped Joseph and Mary, along with Baby Jesus, escape the city before King Herod could find the Christ Child and have him killed. Herod had decreed that all boys under the age of two be massacred in Bethlehem and the surrounding area. But with the shepherd boy's help, the Child Jesus escaped to Egypt. Many years later Jesus, the man, would return the favor and save the shepherd's own son's life when he was gravely ill.

When Zachery was finished, no one spoke for a long while. The poignant story had been spellbinding. Scott finally broke the silence. "Where did you hear that story, Zachery?"

"Long ago, someone told me."

"Is it true?"

"I believe it is."

Scott's eyes were filled with wonder. "Boy, I'll never think of the shepherds in the same way again."

"Wouldn't it be wonderful to add Zachery's legend to our Christmas pageant," Ellen suggested.

"Could we do that, Zachery?" Scott asked.

"I don't see why not. Do you think you could write the script?"

Scott contemplated the idea. "I'd like to try!"

Ellen was still thinking about the story. "So the shepherd boy helped save Jesus' life and, later, Jesus saved the grown shepherd's son? That's amazing."

Zachery nodded. "It allowed the Messiah to demonstrate the *Law of Reciprocity.*"

"What do you mean?"

"The Law of Reciprocity is the spiritual law that governs the 'Golden Rule.' It's our reward for doing unto others *first*. Like what you experienced today. You befriended the Fincastles, then returned home tonight to hear the wonderful news about Jenny."

Scott studied his friend. "Does that mean my sister is going to recover, Zachery?"

"Don't put Zachery on the spot like that," Ellen shook her head at Scott.

Zachery smiled. "I don't mind. Anyway, I'm not the one who can answer that question, Scott. Just remember that there are laws governing the spirit realm, just as there are laws of physics. You trust gravity to work, don't you?"

Scott nodded.

"Then you can trust the spiritual laws to work too."

For the first time since the accident, Scott felt a peacefulness about his sister. He stifled a yawn, suddenly feeling an exhaustion settle on him.

Ellen realized the day had finally taken its toll. "Son," she prodded him up, "you've got to get to sleep. If you don't, Santa's going to skip over the Reid house tonight."

Scott struggled to his feet. "I've got to put Santa's cookies out first," he muttered. Since he was a young boy, he had left Santa a plate of molasses cookies on Christmas Eve. Except last year. After the accident, he hadn't wanted to do it.

But with what had happened tonight, he wasn't about to neglect his traditional duty.

"Don't forget the milk," his father called, as Scott dragged himself to the kitchen.

"Sure, Dad," Scott laughed.

"Poor thing, he's dead tired," Ellen said.

"He's not the only one," Max yawned.

Before moving back to the living room, Ellen double checked the monitor on the night table. She kept the matching monitor next to their bed so she could listen out for Jenny at night. Tonight she wanted to make doubly sure she would hear any noise Jenny might make.

Back in the living room, Ellen gathered up the empty mugs, while Max helped to pick up. They were both eager for bed.

"Mind if I read by the fire for a while?" Zachery asked.

Not at all, they said. They were saying good-night to Zachery as Scott came in with Santa's refreshments. As usual, he had a note attached to the plate reminding Santa of what he wanted for Christmas.

"Don't you stay up," Ellen admonished her son with a kiss good-night.

Setting the refreshments on the hearth, Scott plopped into the wing chair across from Zachery, who was busy reading his Dickens' story. Scott thought about the day as he tried to digest its events. The bags of presents left on the Fincastle's porch was still a mystery. He watched Zachery for a few moments with a shrewd gaze before he broke the silence. "I'm curious, Zachery. Did you have anything to do with those presents tonight?"

"Presents?" Zachery looked up from his book.

"The bags left on the Fincastle's porch."

"Good heavens," Zachery chuckled, "what are you saying?"

Scott felt foolish mentioning it. How could Zachery have

had anything to do with it? They had been together all day. Then he remembered noticing Zachery missing at church. "Where did you go during rehearsal tonight? I looked over where you were sitting, and you weren't there."

Zachery thought a minute. "I was probably borrowing a phone to make a call to my home office."

"Oh," Scott shrugged. His imagination was getting the best of him. His thoughts drifted to the Packard. He still wanted to drive Zachery's car. "Why don't we plan to go check on Charity first thing in the morning."

Laying the book on his lap, Zachery's face seemed to sadden. "You know, I will have to be going once Charity's running again. I do have pressing business."

Scott leaned forward and stirred the fire with the poker. "When will you be passing through Richmond again soon?"

"Can't say exactly. I hope so."

"Will you come see us?"

"Of course."

Scott leaned back in his chair. "I wasn't looking forward to this weekend, Zachery. Not until your visit anyway. . ." The flames seemed to be engulfing his thoughts. As he tried to concentrate, dreamlike figures appeared in the fire and moved along the logs. The figures began reenacting the day's events as his eyes slowly closed.

Scott didn't know how long he had been dozing when Zachery nudged him.

"You should be getting to bed," Zachery spoke in a hushed voice. "I finished my book. Here," he held out the leather bound edition of *A Christmas Carol,* "would you like to read it?"

"Sure," Scott replied groggily.

He barely remembered taking the book, plodding up the steps, and putting on his pajamas. He was asleep before his head hit the pillow.

X

It was eight o'clock the next morning when Ellen woke her son. They had all overslept. She watched with amusement as he looked around his room, still groggy eyed. "Don't you remember what day it is?" she asked.

Scott stared at his mother with a blank face, then his eyes popped open. "Christmas!" He flung back the covers and landed on the floor with one motion. She gave a laugh as he rushed past her and bounded down the steps.

His father was stoking a fire as he rounded the turn into the living room. He quickly scanned the room to see if Santa had brought what he wanted. There it was! He could see one end poking out from behind the sofa. He rushed over and worked the yellow kayak out into the middle of the room. It was a *Whitewater!* The exact model he had wanted! He stroked the one-man canoe as he gave it a once over.

"Merry Christmas," his father said with a grin, watching his son from the fireplace. "Looks like you're ready for this summer."

"Was that what you wanted, Scott?" his mother asked from the doorway.

"Yeah, it's perfect!"

"Why don't you go get Zachery. He won't want to miss this."

Scott gave the kayak one last look, then bounded back up the stairs. When Zachery didn't answer after the second knock, he opened the door and peeked inside. The room was empty and the bed made. *That's odd*, he thought. Noticing a present lying on top of the bed, he walked over and picked it up. It was for Jenny. Beside the present lay a small envelope addressed to him. A strange feeling came over him as he pulled out the note and began reading.

> *Dear Scott,*
>
> > *On the chance my car will start, I am taking my leave early. There is a client I really must visit in West Virginia before Christmas Day is over.*
> >
> > *Please give your parents my heartfelt thanks. I will never forget their gracious hospitality.*
> >
> > *I know the "Law of Reciprocity" will return a blessing for your kindness to me. Please keep my Dickens book as a reminder of our Christmas weekend together.*
>
> > > > *Your friend,*
> > > >
> > > > *Zachery*

Still holding the letter, Scott ran to the top of the stairs and called his parents. "Mom, Dad, come quick!"

"What is it?" they said hurrying to the steps.

"Zachery's gone," he said, motioning for them to come up.

Standing inside the guest room, Max and Ellen looked bewildered as they read Zachery's note.

"Well, I'll be . . ." Max whistled.

"He left a present for Jenny. It's on the bed."

Ellen walked over and picked up the present. She held it and stared out the window thoughtfully.

"What do you make of it, Honey?" Max asked.

"I'm not sure." Her voice sounded distant.

Max scratched his head. "I guess he had a client that couldn't wait. He told us as much all along."

"Well, let's see what he gave Jenny," Ellen said, moving back downstairs.

They gathered around Jenny's bed as Ellen carefully removed the wrapping paper. Perplexed that Zachery had left without saying good-bye, they were now curious to see what was inside.

Ellen gasped as she lifted out an ornately carved silver bell. "I've never seen a bell so beautiful or unusual."

"How in the world could Zachery have known Jenny likes bells?" Scott asked, his eyes wide with surprise.

Ellen shook her head, mystified. "Last night, while the two of you were talking, I showed him Jenny's collection. But there was no way he could have had the opportunity. . ."

Scott took the bell and held it close to his sister's ear. "Listen, Jenny," he said, ringing the bell.

Scott's eyes grew wide. *Had he just seen*—? This time he leaned closer to watch as he rang the bell. *Yes! Jenny's eyelids were moving as if she was trying to open them!* "She's trying to wake up!" he exclaimed.

Everyone froze as Jenny blinked then opened her eyes. The first person she focused on was her brother. "Hi, Scott," she said weakly.

"Jenny, you're okay!" Scott shouted, jumping up and down.

Ellen flung her arms around her daughter, while Max hugged his wife and daughter at the same time. "You're back!" Ellen held Jenny tightly, tears streaming down her cheeks.

"Is something wrong, Mommy?"

Ellen pulled back and studied her daughter's face. "Don't you remember anything, Honey?"

Jenny closed her eyes as she tried to concentrate. "I remember swinging in a playground and there was music playing. A nice man in a red vest was there too, and he was swinging me." Jenny's face broke into a smile. "We were having lots of fun!

"Then I heard a bell ringing. It got louder and louder. Finally the man pulled out a big gold watch and said it was time to go. He took my hand and walked me home. The last thing I remember is coming through our front door." Opening her eyes, Jenny looked around, puzzled. "Why am I in bed? Was I dreaming?"

Ellen stroked her daughter's hair. "Everything is fine now."

Something Jenny said about the man in her dream gave Scott the same odd sensation he had when he first saw Zachery at the Food-Krop. "Jenny, what did the man in your dreams look like?"

"He had white hair, and bushy eyebrows that looked like—"

"Like cotton?"

"Yes," she giggled.

Scott felt his skin tingle. He glanced at his father who had picked up the bell and was now examining it closely. Something was wrong. His father's face had turned pale.

"What is it, Dad?" Scott asked, alarmed.

Max's voice quivered. "I don't understand. This looks like the bell—the present—I gave *her* that day."

"Who, Dad?"

The room was quiet as Max hung onto the bedpost for balance. He seemed disoriented. "Grandnanna. It was the day Grandnanna died. I'll never forget that day. It was during Christmas break, and I was playing basketball that afternoon. A man who I had never seen before came to the gym to say Grandnanna had taken sick. I was to go to the hospital immediately, he said. He gave me a ride, dropped me outside, and told me her room number. I was getting out of the car when he handed me a present, saying it was for her.

"My parents, your Oma and Opa, were already there when I walked into the hospital room. They wanted to know how I knew to come, since there had not been time to notify the school. When I told them about the man, they were puzzled. No one knew anything about him.

"While I was trying to explain about the present, Grandnanna motioned me over to her bedside and had me open the gift. Inside was a bell that looked just like this one!"

Scott gazed at the bell with new interest.

"When Grandnanna saw the bell, she just smiled and whispered that it was an angel who had brought me to the hospital. With a voice so weak I could barely hear, she explained that as a little girl she had heard a legend attached to our family: How, in times of past crisis, our family had been visited by a stranger who, afterward, left a bell. Some said he was an angel."

Scott noticed his father's eyes looked glazed.

"I admit I never put much stock in Grandnanna's story before," Max pondered as he gently fingered the bell. "I guess that's why she loved collecting bells so much."

"What happened next, Dad?" Scott asked.

"Grandnanna drifted off soon afterward holding the bell and wearing the most peaceful smile. Later, when I went outside to look for the man, he was gone. Whoever he was has remained a mystery to this day. I never saw him again."

Max's eyes were moist. "But it was because of him that I got to tell Grandnanna good-bye."

"Was this Grandnanna's bell, Daddy?" Jenny asked, reaching for the bell.

"I'm not sure." Turning to Ellen, Max still looked baffled. "I always wondered what became of that bell. How could Zachery have . . . ?"

Ellen thought she was beginning to understand.

"Dad," Scott asked, "do you remember what kind of car the man was driving when he carried you to the hospital?"

His father's brow wrinkled as he tried to remember, then his eyes grew big. "Why, it was a Packard!" Max's jaw dropped in disbelief as he realized what he was saying. "Well, I'll be. That's why Zachery's face looked so familiar. But that was twenty-five years ago, and he looked the same then as this weekend!"

Scott turned to look out the window as he tried to piece everything together. Suddenly he noticed the change of weather and hollered, "Hey, it's starting to snow! We're going to have a white Christmas after all!"

"You mean it's Christmas?" Jenny asked excitedly.

They nodded and helped her sit up so she could see.

After a minute, Jenny looked back at them puzzled. "Who is *Zachery?*"

Ellen smiled at her daughter. "He was a very special stranger who visited us this weekend."

Scott was shaking his head. "But who was Zachery *really?*"

"Just a minute and I'll tell you." Ellen's face seemed to glow as she reached over to the night stand to pick up the Bible. She found the passage she was looking for and began reading.

*Don't forget to be kind to strangers, for some who have done this have entertained angels without realizing it!**

Now Scott understood.

"I want to hear about Zachery!" Jenny said impatiently.

Scott smiled. Already, his sister was sounding like the Jenny he remembered.

"You tell her, Scott," his folks nodded.

"Okay," Scott said, climbing onto Jenny's bed. "Settle back and enjoy the snow, Little Sister, while I tell you about our family's *special guest.*"

THE END

*Scripture can be found in Hebrews 13:2. The verse was quoted from The Living Bible.